BARBIE™: A Fairy-Tale Mermaid

A CENTUM BOOK 978-1-914448-36-2

Published in Great Britain by Centum Books Ltd.

This edition published 2021.

1 3 5 7 9 10 8 6 4 2

books@centumbooksltd.co.uk

CENTUM BOOKS LIMITED. Reg. No. 07641486

A CIP catalogue record for this book is available
from the British Library.

Printed in Great Britain.

Barbie™

A Fairy-Tale Mermaid

This is my book.
My name is

....

centum

Merliah Summers couldn't have been happier. She had just won the big Malibu surfing competition – which meant she would soon be going to the World Championship Surfing Invitational in Australia!

'You were lucky, mate,' sneered Kylie Morgan, Merliah's biggest rival. 'But your luck's gonna run out down under – that's *my* turf.'

Merliah couldn't wait to tell her mother the good news. Swimming out into the ocean, she held her magic necklace tight and said, 'I wish to become a mermaid.' Suddenly, the young surfer's legs were transformed into a beautiful tail. Merliah had a secret – she was a mermaid princess! Her mother was Queen Calissa, ruler of the enchanted underwater kingdom of Oceana.

After congratulating her daughter for winning the surfing competition, the queen invited Merliah to the very important Changing of the Tides ceremony. Every twenty years, a member of the royal family sat on the ancient throne to regain the power to make Merillia, the life force of the ocean.

Merliah couldn't participate in the Changing of the Tides ceremony. If she did, she would lose forever her ability to change back into a human. But Calissa thought it was Merliah's duty to at least attend the ceremony. Unfortunately, it was on the same day as the surfing competition, and Merliah was determined to be there instead. The queen was very disappointed.

Kylie won the first round of the World Championship Surfing Invitational, but Merliah received all the attention from the reporters and fans. She had performed a handstand on her board during her run!

'But I won!' Kylie exclaimed angrily.

As Kylie fumed on the beach, a talking rainbow fish named Alistair suddenly appeared beside her. Alistair told Kylie that the secret to Merliah's success was her magic necklace. So Kylie stole the necklace and used it to turn into a mermaid. Then Alistair promised to take Kylie to someone who could teach her the secrets of surfing.

Alistair led Kylie down to the bottom of the ocean. Suddenly, the fish pushed the young surfer into a whirlpool! Kylie became trapped and Queen Calissa's evil sister, Eris, was released. Months before, Eris had been imprisoned in the whirlpool for trying to take over Oceana. Now free, the wicked mermaid was going to try again, at the Changing of the Tides ceremony!

Luckily, Merliah's sea lion friend, Snouts, had seen what had happened to Kylie. Swimming as fast as he could, Snouts found Merliah and led her to the whirlpool. Together they rescued Kylie.

'I never should have taken your necklace,' Kylie said. 'And if your aunt is going to hurt the ocean, I want to help stop her.'

Meanwhile, as she was preparing tea for the Changing of the Tides ceremony, Calissa heard a chilling voice. 'You're not setting a place for me?' Eris asked.

The evil mermaid cast a spell on her sister, and Calissa's worst nightmare came true – her tail turned to stone! Helpless, the queen sank to the ocean floor.

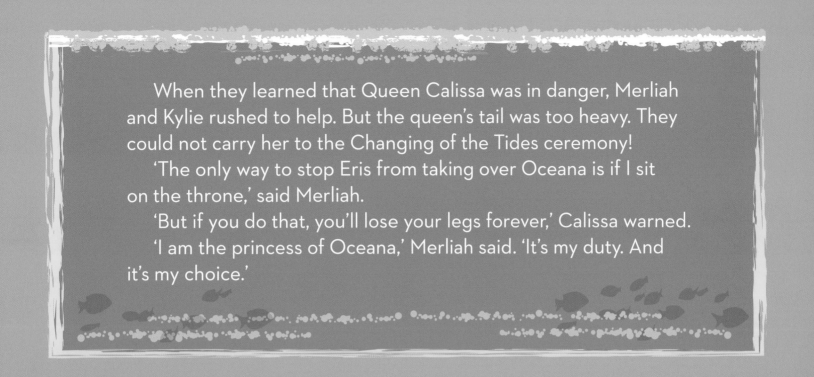

When they learned that Queen Calissa was in danger, Merliah and Kylie rushed to help. But the queen's tail was too heavy. They could not carry her to the Changing of the Tides ceremony!

'The only way to stop Eris from taking over Oceana is if I sit on the throne,' said Merliah.

'But if you do that, you'll lose your legs forever,' Calissa warned.

'I am the princess of Oceana,' Merliah said. 'It's my duty. And it's my choice.'

Merliah and Kylie raced to the Changing of the Tides ceremony and knocked Eris off the throne. Merliah sat on the throne, but when the magical lights of the Changing of the Tides shone down on her, nothing happened.

'You have no tail!' Eris said, cackling. 'You can't activate the throne!'

Realising what she had to do, Kylie took a deep breath. She quickly took the magic necklace from her own neck and put it around Merliah's.

'I wish to become a mermaid,' Merliah declared. Suddenly, her legs transformed into a glorious mermaid's tail and the throne was bathed in colourful glowing lights. Merliah had stopped Eris and gained the power to make Merillia! Oceana was saved!

'Nooo!' Eris cried. She tried to cast a nightmare spell on Merliah, but the spell bounced off the throne and hit Eris instead. The evil mermaid's worst nightmare came true – she had human legs!

Merliah was happy to have saved Oceana, but she was sad that she could no longer surf. As she and her mother swam back to the surface with Kylie, magical light swirled around her and her tail turned back into legs!

'The ceremony must have transformed you into your truest self,' Calissa explained. 'You are both a mermaid *and* a human.'

'Now you can surf in the meet!' exclaimed Kylie. 'Come on!'

Later, as the two friends rode the waves, Merliah forgot all about the competition. She was too busy creating glistening Merillia. 'I'm loving this!'

Kylie won the competition, and Merliah was very happy for her. But more importantly, Merliah realised how lucky she was to have good friends and family, above and below the sea.

Reading tips

We hope you and your child enjoy reading this picture book.

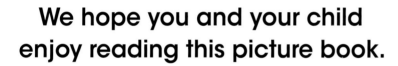 Try to make time to read with your child every day and make reading together something you both look forward to.

A good way to bring a book to life is to put on different voices for different characters in the story.

You could also stop at certain points in the book to ask your child what they think about the characters, what is happening in the story and what they think might happen next.

You can still read aloud to your child, even when they are confident enough to read by themselves.

If your child is excited about the subject they are reading about, it will help them to retain their interest in reading.

A love of reading can last a lifetime!